good deed rain

FLOP

FLOP © 2024
Allen Frost, Good Deed Rain
Bellingham, Washington
ISBN: 979-8-3305-7550-3

Writing & Drawings: Allen Frost
Cover Photo of author's actual art installation in the WWU Fine Arts B Gallery. The show lasted for less than five minutes in the summer of 2024.
Cover Production: Robert Millis
Quote:
Ruth Gordon, *Columbo*, Season 7, Ep.1, 1977.
Apple: TFK!

FLOP

Allen Frost

Good Deed Rain ◊ Bellingham, Washington ◊ 2024

"I accept all superlatives."
—Ruth Gordon

CHAPTERS

Beckett	19
These Houses by the Sea	23
A Picture in My Mind	27
A Deal on a Seal	31
Avocados	37
A Can of Rain	40
The Same as Yesterday	43
The Cascades in a Radio	46
Below the Beehive	49
Famous	53
Buttercup Things	56
Pterodactyl Duty	58
This Day and Age	63
Happy Wednesday	66

Time Takes Care of Everything	69
Holly Street Hero	73
What Comes Back	76
Champion of My Imaginary Gameshow	79
Compared with the Ocean	83
The Gallery Calls	87
Amelia Earhart	90
Condemned	94
Ghost Directions	96
A Rainy-Day Song	99
Another Seashell	102
The Magic Planet	105
More than a Dime	108
Where We Are	111
The Gift	114
Mercy	117
My Taxi	120

I exist precariously with another world called imagination.

INTRODUCTION

When I was four feet tall, I was another person, only ten years old and this world was still a new planet. I was lucky enough to be surrounded by plenty of strange wonders in a colorful Seattle in the 1970s. [*Read *The Tin Can Telephone* for more.] In the University District, on Brooklyn Avenue next to The Outrageous Taco, was a little shop with curtains and incense and a *PLOP* comic in the window. The cover was so bright and crazy it caught my attention and found a spot in my memory.

I don't know if it was time travel, but when that title came back to me this spring, it was easy to turn Plop into Flop and make a new book out of something long-gone. There's a lot of time travel going on in this book, but let's face it, do we really want to go backwards when we're here in the now and there's so much we can do to make things better?

shows come and go

As I grew, for some reason I found myself haunted, doing time in comic book warehouses, odd studios, and for the last ten years a job in an art department office.

At work there's a gallery where the shows come and go until school ends and the room becomes empty. I told Janet that's when I'm going to install my show: The Same As Yesterday. Nothing will happen in there. Defying the fundamental principle of the universe, this space will remain unchanged. For a little while that was true. And as you can see from the cover, the exhibition was quite the event of the summer. In other words, a flop.

—AF, July 13, 2024

BECKETT

Of course it goes to figure they would have seals as pets. It makes sense, with that much beach and ocean in front of you. When Gloria asked me to seal-sit, I didn't think it would come to this—me, standing up in a pitching rowboat calling "Beckett!" over and over. But there you have it. It didn't have to happen that way, but it did.

I was careful. I put the harness on Beckett before we left the house. I made sure it was tight but not too tight and the leash was attached, and the end was looped in my hand. When I opened the door, I led the way aware to keep the seal by my side. Gloria warned me, he's going to pull you, he wants to get in that water more than anything in the world. She was right. Holding onto that leash was like hanging on to a waterski towline.

I was pretty much dragged to the shore, to the rowboat that waited in the sand above where the tide could reach. Beckett knew the routine. He lurched to the boat and looked over his shoulder and arfed at me. "Okay, okay," I said.

It's hard to imagine Gloria going through this every day, but she must have a little more control over the rambunctious seal. I clipped his leash to the eyelet on the rope connected to the bow and quickly stepped into the boat. The second I let go, we were on the move. It was a good thing I was sitting down. Beckett pulled the boat like a sled across the hushing sand.

Why have a seal as a pet? Why not a simpler, smaller creature? A sea urchin would do me fine. Crawling in meticulous slow-motion in a bowl. If I wanted, I could hold it on my palm like a spiky flower, but mostly I'd let it be, glad for the company.

Beckett thrashed into the water like an eggbeater, flippers and fins splashing and then he was submerged and the powerful beast was a *Nautilus* motor. You could ride bicycle wheels on that taut tightrope. It didn't take long to get past the breaking waves, out deep into the gentle swells. That's where I release the brake lock on the rope and let Beckett run. The rope sings from a big wooden reel mounted in the bow, whirring from the spool as the seal chases fish, twisting, turning, like a swallow above a field.

There are times when you'll see other boats attached to seals, when people get home from work, or at dawn before the first trolley takes them there. It's a long day for a seal stuck at home. Today I was alone at sea. The sound of the rope rubbing wood, the water lapping on the hull.

Lucky for Beckett, I don't have one of those jobs where I fall into a clock until the sun goes down. I'm here all day. We go out here a few times, in the morning and the afternoon. Yesterday it was raining and I watched the raindrops peck the ocean. The sky was typing on it. Then I thought of the water as a canvas put on a wall and the rain was what the brush was telling us. I wondered if I could do something like that. After a while, Beckett's face reappeared in the air and he wanted to play.

A yellow tennis ball rolled a little by my feet. "Hang on, Beckett." I ducked out of sight and got the ball. Beckett's wet eyes were riveted to it, and he pitched his head back and barked. I drew my arm back and threw. Off he went. Followed by a few more fathoms of rope. Beckett popped up directly under the ball and caught it as it dropped from the air like an apple.

When there's more than one seal around, they swim to each other and tangle. There's a seal named Yo-Yo who's sort of a terror. The appearance of their rowboat is like a pirate ship. If we're on the water and I spot it I'll turn around, bend into the oars, trying to keep as much distance as I can.

Beckett paddled close and flipped the ball to me. Gloria told me he can do this all day, but he does get tired after a while. Even a chattering windup toy will run out of steam. Halfway to another throw, he got distracted and dived. I've seen him go after a salmon and catch it. The spool responded with more humming rope. I could put the brake on and pull him up if I had to, but this is good exercise for him. It beats drooping in a kid's blue wading pool at home, next to the window and the radiator. I'm surprised Gloria doesn't have a big saltwater pool installed, but she's got the whole ocean in front of her. The little blue pool just keeps Beckett from drying out, the way a flower needs a vase.

THESE HOUSES by the SEA

While Beckett submarined, I rowed ahead to collect the tennis ball. I lost one last week. It's probably on its way to Guam. The reel continued to click out line. It rarely ran to the end. There was enough rope to run through a mansion. Below the surface he could be entering room after room. Beckett was in another world tied to me by only a string. I thought about doing a painting, a dream scene someone is in, like Beckett underwater, and they're tied to a cord that winds out of the frame and you can pull them back into three-dimensions. I don't know how you could manage that, I don't know if it makes any sense, but I was turning the idea over. Paintings like water you can reach into. I thought about how the B Minus Gallery would look. I let the oar drag against the current while I reached out and got the floating ball.

The rope went slack. I gave a pull. There was no weight to it.

The boat had no Beckett anchor.

I didn't want to panic. I reeled in the loose wet line. Up it came much too easily. All the way to where I could see the white end of it twirling in the green water. It had been cut. No Beckett.

What if he was stuck in a giant clam, or slammed in a treasure chest? A shark? An orca? No, no. Careful, I told myself, don't get carried away. I exist precariously with another world called imagination.

Slid under the board seat in the stern is a toolbox. You wouldn't expect a need for too many tools in a rowboat that just goes back and forth from the shore. I opened the box and got a telescope and a bell. I left the can of sardines. They were a last resort if Beckett refused to get in the boat. So far during my seal-sitting venture I haven't had any trouble with Beckett. He's friendly and amusing. I understand the appeal of a seal. I don't live where I could have one, no waterfront mansion for me, the best I could do for a seal is a clawfoot bathtub filled with Epsom salt, and if I got a shopping cart, I could buggy the seal to Green Lake for a swim.

First, I stuck my hand beneath the surface and I rang the bell underwater. It was supposed to bring him back right away. Gloria trained him that way. If he shot to the top, I would get the sardines, but the rope was snapped as a bridge cable. My sleeve was drenched. I couldn't hear the bell in the middle of a wave but I'm sure its ringing didn't go unnoticed. Beckett was hiding down there looking up at me from the depths daring me to do something more. A bubble rising my way like a jellyfish was his answer. Fine.

I lifted the bell from the water and clattered it beside my feet. I shook off my arm. Soaked. Time for the telescope. It was fun to watch Beckett play, if only there was a way to attach a paintbrush to him when he's off on a jaunt. I'd love to see that calligraphy.

There wasn't any. Not that I could see at first. I searched the kelp forest. It swirled in curtains. Kelp didn't help. I turned the lens over that pinnacle of rock where the kelp grew and focused past, going further down.

The telescope showed me only murk.

What's the point of the suspense? You already

know I'm standing in the boat calling his name. Let's just jump to that.

"Beckett!" I knew it was hopeless. I sat down. The boat steadied. The ocean can stretch as far as you can imagine. It ran through my mind: What if Beckett is gone? Here it was, my last day of seal-sitting and I was picking up Gloria at the airport tonight and bringing her to a home without a seal. I was in trouble.

Drifting, holding the oars calling "Beckett" one last time in view of these houses by the sea.

A PICTURE in MY MIND

I pulled the boat back to its place on shore, stopped in the sand, stowed the oars, and I left it there in the beachgrass. Peaceful. It could be a painting on a hotel wall. Beautiful. If only that big fishing reel in the bow wasn't empty. I turned around and took one more look at the ocean. A calm morning at sea. Then I went to the house, Gloria's house, and got the car keys.

Despite this calamity, I have things to do. Places to be. In the meantime, I would look for a seal on land.

Win some, lose some. I'm used to it.

Besides, how can you have a pet seal anyway? It's like holding onto a flying fish. Beckett must be happier where he is now. He chose his path, but I let him go. Aw gee, what am I supposed to tell Gloria? I don't know...That can wait.

Maybe something will work out.

She must have known there was this side to me when she asked for my help. I'm good, but only so far. Oh gee, I wish I was more dependable. I'm not. Not everything goes my way. I try. I don't know why she chose me to watch her seal, it was a mistake for her to ask and a mistake for me to accept. I'm sorry. That's what I'll say. That's the way it goes.

I'll buy her some flowers.

Then again, she's probably received a thousand of those at the festival. She'll be coming home wrapped up in them. Bees and hummingbirds will be orbiting her. When I was at the grocery store yesterday, I saw her on the cover of a tabloid. Glorious Gloria. Movie star. After her reception in France, will Beckett be such a tragedy?

I pressed the red button on the key fob and the garage door raised. Sunshine slipped over the Nash Statesman 600. What a sleek and slippery car. It looked made for moon travel.

It's entirely possible that when I return, Beckett will be waiting. Maybe he just needed a little time away, maybe he'll miss his swimming pool by the window and fish from a can. These pampered seals that live in houses along the beach have got it made. I put a picture in my mind of Beckett sitting on the deck when I got back, and I steered out of the garage onto the gravel driveway, between palm trees to the gate, to the road where I turned right.

The B Minus Gallery isn't far. The traffic was light. A pterodactyl drifted in the blue sky, taking its time toward the hills.

stamped in a factory

A DEAL on a SEAL

I happened to find a parking spot right in front of Peckinpaw's Pet Shop.
  Was this preordained? Do I go in and get a new seal? A shadow I could fool her with for a while. Will Gloria know the difference? She will. This isn't a screwball comedy. Beckett comes back from the sea to find his twin taking his place? I'll avoid that plot. A living creature is not stamped in a factory. Every living thing is unique. Face it, even a rock is too. You can't find two that are the same. Maybe it's only people who want to create the same thing over and over. Clones are all the rage. I worked in a factory with two of them—Marv and, oh, I forget the other one's name—we were on the line making the same parts of a town over and over every day. We made the streets and stores, lampposts and signs, and rolled it all up in a tube to put in a rocket. Next stop Mars, or some

other planet. When people get there, it'll be just like home.

Funny, having said all that, it might help understand my show at the B Minus Gallery. If it needs explanation...You'll see.

A dog was barking in Peckinpaw's. I opened the door and went inside. One of the first things you notice in a pet store is the smell. It would be the same aroma aboard Noah's ark. And there were cages and glass cases and aquariums in every space. A parrot swung on a small trapeze. A vivarium of butterflies shook like autumn leaves. I squeezed into an aisle full of snakes and spiders and hurried through.

The lights got dim at the back of the shop, that's where I was headed, I've been here before. Last week I bought seal vitamins. Beckett was running low.

A horse watched me from a hole cut in the wall. It stretched its neck down to pull at some hay. I'm sure the Peckinpaw people spend most of the day feeding their animals. And what about at night? Who feeds the bats and raccoons when the lights go out? I don't know, I just want to see if there's a deal on a seal.

I went by a barrel labeled Crickets. It was full of them, a whole town of them. They crawled all around up to the clear plastic lid. A scoop rested on top, and there were paper bags you could pour them in, popping about inside. I said, "Hiya Jiminy." One of them had to be him, right? But I don't know if I could use his kind of help—do I really need someone telling me every time I do something wrong? I'm full of mistakes. I don't need another conscience, one is plenty.

The air got cooler as I stepped down four stairs into the midst of aquariums. Blue and green water bubbled and chirped. Tropical fish in unbelievable shapes, colors, sizes. A couple kids, sister and brother I guessed, were getting help picking two goldfish from a tank. This was a little like my idea for art you can reach into. The aquariums got bigger, one of them held a school of mackerel that turned like pouring silver dimes. An octopus. A sea turtle. Far in the distance I saw a shadow that looked like a whale.

"Can I help you?" one of the employees asked.

"I think I'm getting there," I said. "I'm thinking about a seal."

She said, "Sure, follow me."

Are car dealerships set up this way? Is this how Gloria got her Nash? I don't know, cars are out of my budget, so are seals come to think of it. Maybe I could get one on trade? I could paint the Tradewinds on the ceiling or the Gulfstream swirling on the floor.

A shark swam in the glass beside us. I sure don't want one of those.

"Have you ever had a seal?" the girl asked me.

"Yes. I've got one now. They're great." What was I supposed to say?

"You'd like a companion for it?"

"That's right." I don't know what was in the next tank, it was full of swaying kelp.

We stopped at the next window. A piece of paper was taped to it. Sold Out.

"Oh dear, I'm sorry," she said. "Would you like me to put your name on a list?"

"No, that's okay. I was hoping for a seal, but for now I'll take a sea urchin."

"Those are way back at the start," she told me, and we turned around.

That was fine. I had a few dollars in my pocket. Hopefully that would cover it. It did. Gloria would be happy. It looked like a flower in the clear tied bag. What a simple creature to care for. I even had change left over for a shaker can of diatoms to feed it. When I got back to the beach house, I would dip some fresh seawater in a bucket and pour it in a glass vase. I can't understand why you'd want anything else.

getting a sandwich

AVOCADOS

Maybe I'm no better than that Peckinpaw shark. I left the pet shop feeling hungry. The gallery was just across the street but all I could think about was getting a sandwich from Pearl's. So that's what I did, lured to the next block and around the corner. I won't go into a lot of sandwich detail. It wouldn't be fair, especially for someone reading this who is hungry. I can picture you. Just the string of a few words like "avocado and red onions and mustard" is enough for you to set this book down. You've seen enough. Avocado! The nerve of that suggestion. Your kitchen hasn't entertained an avocado in months. Your Stop 'n Shop is millions of miles from the sunny land where avocados grow, but maybe a rocket is on the way. Stocked with fruit and vegetables from Earth. Oh, the ones on Mars are okay, they take some getting used to, but there's nothing like a fresh California orange.

You push the window curtain and look at the pink sky. Did a rocket just land? You're obsessed with avocados now! Why wait? The rustberries in the clay bowl on the counter need to be tossed out on the sand and replaced by 'Still Life with Avocado.' You can hop on a coaster and get to the grocery in ten minutes, but you went to the phone instead. There's a phone installed on every kitchen wall. I know your kitchen, remember, I made them in the factory. I also know there's a phonebook. You take the receiver and dial the Stop 'n Shop number. If you rode all the way there and they didn't have avocados, you might just keep riding, to the rocket landing, to stowaway on the next flight to Earth. You get the cashier at register #3 who transfers you to the produce manager, a man named Jemp who has lived on Mars for fourteen years. He likes it here, he likes the rustberries, and gorfbark, and the sour leaves that bloom on quicksand. He wants everyone to love them as much as him, he takes time to display them in pyramids, and he marks prices down once a week. If any shopper looks puzzled, Jemp is quick to give suggestions for recipes. And yet, every week, there are people like you who want a watermelon, or a crisp red apple and he repeats what he always repeats: "we're on Mars now, we have to adapt." You know, you've heard that before, but you also know there are other ways. There's always been an underworld, even on this world, another planet, where you can get what you want for a price. What would it cost you for an avocado sold in some fractured Martian alley and would it be worth it? Oh, you're a hundred million miles away but I know you, I see you, I feel your struggle. I have no trouble imagining you. These are the people I'm reaching out to. When I mention avocado ten times, it's a signal as real as a drumbeat, as real as a brush painting green. This is the spell I cast, while night falls on Mars, on a book with an unexplained sandwich.

A CAN of RAIN

I don't exactly make a living as an artist. I don't think I could afford a pound of rice on what I pull in a week. If it wasn't for the seal-sitting job, I'd be out beating the streets. Speaking of which, I just stopped by Cellophane Square. There's newspaper taped over the glass. It's closing! I can't believe it—what will happen to all that music? Sometime during the night, the records will shed their sleeves and all the black vinyl will become the feathers of a huge bird that will break through the roof and fly over 42nd Street. It will sing somewhere else. Maybe the moon.

I can't believe our survival depends on money. Why not something real, like rain in a bucket? Everyone has the same chance and gets no more or less than your neighbor's bucket can hold. We'd look forward to cloudy days and don't forget to put some in the bank for an unrainy day. Money is just as abstract and far more cruel. Good people can't make it, and good ideas like record stores come and go. Flap, flap, a black nightbird knocks down more rain from a cloud.

 I've had to look for ways to live my life without a rain bucket. I check in once a week with Labor Now. Before Gloria called me, the agency told me they had a great job, perfect for an artist like me. That sounded alright, better than a factory. Until I went to the Aurora Bridge and found out what I was meant to do. They gave me paint and brushes. It was a good start. Then they told me to paint over the graffiti. It was all over the cement pillars. The paint in the can was gray as a raincloud. I'm supposed to drown out all these words and pictures while the noise and colors of the cars roar above. Then if I do a good job, they'll move me to another spot. That will be my contribution, to keep the city painted gray. Forget it. I sat on a can of paint and waited for the end of the day.

 It's a good thing Gloria got in touch. Thanks to her generosity I know I'll get by. What I do may not be noticed by the world at large, but like one of those old-time magicians on a wooden stage, I'm going to keep pulling a rabbit out of a hat.

Which brings me to the B Minus Gallery and my new installation that opened last night: The Same as Yesterday.

The SAME as YESTERDAY

Laika met me at the doorway with a small flower. On Mondays she greets everyone this way, that's her custom, she's a Mondayist.

I said, "Hi Laika."

"Happy Monday!" she smiled.

She's got a big job making people happy on Mondays. It isn't easy. Most people get Saturday and Sunday off, and Monday looks like the tarpit start of a deep workweek. Mondayists want to turn that perception around. I wish them good luck. I took the daisy from her and tucked it into my shirt pocket. "Come in," she said. Laika also owns the B Minus Gallery. "Welcome to The Same as Yesterday."

The gallery was empty.

In a way. It depends on your point of view.

There's white paint on the walls, there's a ceiling with lights shining down. Shadows.

It's meant to be calm. You take a breath and step inside a stillness that stays the same. Nothing is happening and you stay the same with it. I know change is everywhere, I know by now it can't be stopped, but this is supposed to be a place where it does.

Laika sat at her table by the door. The tabletop has been neatly stacked with brochures and flyers. A jar of flowers. A book. A folded *Herald*. I wondered if there was a review of my reception. Laika would tell me if there was. Unless it was bad. The guestbook was open and the pages were white as snow.

I crossed the gallery. The Same as Yesterday. I heard Laika's chair creak. She picked up a book. I knew it was next to a jar full of daisies, but they were too quiet to hear. There were other sounds too, sounds never stop. The #372 bus on its route. Cars are always in the background. Sparrows in the leaves. The sounds made a mobile turning in the room.

My show would be up for a week. Next week there's a new one, and Laika scheduled me for another too. I looked at the same and wondered what I'd do.

I thought about the Cellophane Square bird. I could suspend it in here with record wings that curved up to the ceiling. Eyes that were 45s. A victrola beak. The ten thousand grooves dug into it shine and maybe as it spins very slowly you will recognize a song.

Then, as always happens sooner or later, the calm was broken. That giant black bird idea was knocked down by something new. A new sound. I turned around.

Outside. Suddenly it started raining so hard I had to go look. All that water was carried in the sky just a minute ago and all at once it decided it wanted to fall and cover the ground and when it wanted to, it would stop.

The CASCADES in a RADIO

I stood in the doorway frame close enough to reach my hand into the rain. It was falling heavily in a silver curtain, making the raindrops bounce high off the sidewalk. Really coming down. It's the sort of a rain that won't last long, not the steady drizzle we get most of the winter. A rare animal. I wondered where it came from, cut like cake from a cloud over Annapurna. I could hear the little bells on yaks, I could smell the ocean it must have traveled over, clean and cool. There was a great moment when it began raining even harder. The roar filled the gutters with streams. Ahhh, rain is a wonderful, wonderful sound. Think of all the ways water likes to run, over the ground, in lakes and seas, rivers, in the air. Then a dial was turned, and the volume slowly hushed. I could hear the city recovering. A waterspout pinging like sonar. I stood in the doorway and listened to the music.

My eyes were shut. I opened them.

We live between mountains in a plain and we're used to rain. The Olympics to the west, and the Cascades to the east. Those peaks are usually visible between the buildings and trees but not when everything is gray. The rain wasn't quite done, though it was weakening. I remembered an old song that used to play. When I was little, I pretended there were real people inside the radio. They lived small lives just to sing. I used to listen to the radio with my grandparents and their channel played big band and crooners. I came to learn the radio is adapting to its audience. Another generation was taking over, tuning in, wanting to hear their songs, and Nat King Cole became rock'n'roll. The Cascades were on the radio in their heyday, becoming more endangered in the airwaves as the years went by, then becoming an extinct bird—if you want to know what the fabled blue-throated wren sounded like, find a jukebox with that 1962 love song to the rain.

On my hand, the rain got fine as beach sand, a gentle prickling on skin like the dew rolling over the tops of grass, the sigh in all that exists. The wet street was tipping back to the sea cupping

Cellophane Square, The Doghouse, The Globe Café, Beauty and the Books, The Newsstand, Crazy Mike's Video, carried like paper boats in a creek. The door was open behind me. The Same as Yesterday slipped past me and joined the parade.

There isn't a day goes by I'm not reminded of something that used to be. It's like I said before, the things that disappear stay inside you, the way a tree holds rings. They were here to be my inspiration. I only miss what left me who I am, but I don't want to bring all those shadows back. I'm not looking for time travel. If you go further, everything was cedars, and long before that were the dinosaurs.

BELOW the BEEHIVE

When I couldn't see rain anymore, only what it left behind, wet streets and pools, I picked up a bee that was stuck in a puddle. There are hundreds of them living upstairs. Caught in the downpour, the poor honeybee nearly drowned. I put him on my shirt cuff and smoothed the bee's wings and wet yellow and black coat.

Funny, the ocean is a mirror of our world, where there are dogfish, catfish, mermaids, fish with wings and legs, sea cows, seahorses, sea cucumbers, kelp forests, flowers, and I'm sure there are bee-fish under there too. Who knows, I only float atop it.

Before getting to Laika's desk I turned up the stairway that leads from The B Minus Gallery to Marlin's apartment upstairs. The bee stayed still on my arm. It makes you wonder what they do when it rains. They must be aware before it happens so they can look for shelter. Not this one though, he wasn't paying attention to the bee radio warnings. He went out looking for flowers the same as usual but when he hit the weather he only got as far as the sidewalk. Good thing I happened by.

About halfway up the stairs, you feel a change, almost ominous like the Sargasso Sea approaching. I never left the stairway before. Laika did once. She opened the door. The electric humming is a gigantic honeycomb that fills the room from wall to wall.

I made it to the top of the stairs. If I was seven it might have been far enough, I would have run from the landing, but I'm not afraid of bees. Even if behind the door there's a beehive that resembles Chicago.

The landing was dark, the overhead lightbulb was out, but it didn't matter, a golden light beamed at me from the keyhole.

I hoped the returning bee would be welcomed. "We were looking everywhere for you!" I hoped he wouldn't feel like a heel for going out in the rain. It was only a mistake. Then again, maybe he wasn't missed, maybe he'll go past the crowds and into his wax apartment and pull a blanket over his head and fall asleep. Poor bee.

I steered my arm into the light and stopped my hand next to the keyhole. The hum was louder than ever and the gold sunlight was so bright I had to shade my eyes with my other hand.

"Go on," I said. The bee wasn't in a hurry to crawl through the keyhole. He froze in the spotlight.

Who knows, perhaps Marlin rules his bee kingdom like a tyrant. He's in there with a clipboard—"Number 799, you're late!" I do know he made a fortune from the bees. I've only seen him a couple times, he doesn't seem like a tyrant, in fact he seems just the opposite, he's the gallery's patron saint. He signs the checks. The B Minus couldn't afford the telephone bill without him.

The bee finally got the picture and stirred. This isn't their usual way into the apartment, but I wasn't going to climb the fire escape and let him in the window. I said, "Go on. Good luck."

Once a week an armored truck comes to this address. That's how good the honey is. It takes a guard to carry the buckets out. I have a jar at home. It's supposed to make you live to be a hundred. Marlin is almost there. A miracle elixir.

They ought to leave a guard at the door.

The bee was gone. So was I. I left all the gold in the mountain and climbed downstairs, past the desk to the door.

"Happy Monday!" Laika called after me.

FAMOUS

I've been with Gloria when she gets recognized. People confuse her with the characters she plays. It happens all the time. I can't imagine that feeling, well I sort of can. I had my brief moment in the sun. Once in a blue moon someone will remember my claim to fame. I'm not known for being an artist—I was on a TV show called *Where'd It Go?* A studio full of bright lights, three contestants facing the cameras, with me beating the odds day after day.

As I was keying the Nash door someone called me. If I was on the show just once, this wouldn't happen, but I starred for a month. I was either a fan favorite or a villain depending on your view. When I'm recognized I can tell right away if there's going to be trouble.

A car was stopped in the road beside me

and someone leaned out the open window. "My brother says you're Oscar Morris. The guy from the gameshow."

"Yes, that's right."

"Hah, I knew it!" He punched his brother, the guy behind the wheel.

"You're the best!" his brother waved.

"Oh, thanks."

"Hey, what's your secret?" A car behind them honked its horn and he shook his fist.

I get that question a lot. I told him, "I guess I'm just lucky I guess." I don't have any secret to three-card monte, I've just always had that talent to track what's missing.

"When you going back on?"

I said I wasn't. Actually, the station wouldn't let me continue. They had me throw the next game to get rid of me. I didn't explain that though. I signed papers, I'm resigned to secrecy.

Another car horn blatted and my admirer and his brother gave a last salute and the traffic started to move again.

With Gloria, it's different. She's a genuine star. Movies. A movie star. People will see her on the street and you'd think she was Cleopatra.

Flashbulbs. Adoration. I'm glad I lack that notoriety. Since I gave up television for The B Minus Gallery, I'm mostly unremarkable.

BUTTERCUP THINGS

I met Emily Dickinson on Eastlake Avenue. She worked in a bakery. She was talking to Charlie Chaplin. I couldn't help myself—I would stop by every week, I brought her flowers I picked around the neighborhoods, buttercup things and fireweed. I didn't know what I was doing, it must have been the moon, I was just something washing in its current.

The time travel agency Tic Toc Travel brings famous people to-and-fro. Luminaries walk the streets among us. Tic Toc even stacked the air with pterodactyls and put Joan of Arc in the park. We grow accustomed to the migrations of time. We can join the flow. They want us to know time travel is safe and as easy as taking a trolley ride. They have stores in a few locations. Laika still raves about La Belle Époque in Paris. She's saving to go back again. For all my talk about the past, I bet you're surprised I haven't tried. Wouldn't it be fun to visit 1975? One of those childhood summer nights chasing fireflies? No, I don't have to. That's what memories are for. For as long as they last. The fireflies are caught in me in amber.

One time I was riding a bus on Lake City Way, looking out the window, and I saw Dizzy Gillespie. He was dressed in a long wool overcoat, holding a trumpet case, waiting for the light to change so he could cross the street to Safeway.

PTERODACTYL DUTY

I got on the elevator. In the last century they had an operator in a green uniform pressing buttons, pulling levers—in our time there's me, riding up the floors to scare off dinosaurs. That's progress. It's my steady job to keep the pterodactyls off the roof of The Leopold. It doesn't pay. It's for room and board.

At the ninth floor, the door opened and I stepped out onto the worn carpet. I crossed the hall and went close to the red wallpaper where there's a door cut into the pattern. A rectangle seam. I unlocked it, hit the light switch and in the narrow room was a ladder spine with bones that xylophoned up to the ceiling. It wasn't easy carrying my belongings to the roof, but that's where they put me, that's where a dinosaur job will get you. Fortunately, I don't own a piano.

Like a submarine, there's a hatch to fumble

open. When there's rain topside, it's like a pitching sea. What rain was left just ran down my sleeve. I'm pretty sure I won't be doing this too many more years, hopefully when I'm a really old man I'll have something besides a tent a hundred feet from the ground.

For now, I like it here. I'm only a reach from the clouds. I took a deep breath and stretched my arms out. The birds and I know what it's like to live in the air.

The rooftop is a flat plain of vents and chimneys and a few old aerials. The iron stanchion for a radio tower that used to be here. Also, there's one of my big ideas spread out in a jumble on the tar. It was inspired by the elements, the sound of the wind and the rain. Assembled like a symphony awaiting me, there are coffee cans and aluminum bowls, glass jars and bottles, hanging chimes, tin pie plates, pots and pans. I call it The Gamelan Rain Orchestra. When it was pouring an hour ago, the concert would have been amazing. If anyone was around to hear it. I don't have chairs and umbrellas, but there is an audience.

A rabbit hopped and stopped, head turned, a coal-black eye observing me. A garden grows all around the rim of the roof, spinach, kale, clover and the weeds that find their way here. Another rabbit stared at me. Yes, I've introduced rabbits to the skyline. In a few hundred years they may develop wings and fly over the crumbled remains of our civilization.

Which brings me to the pterodactyls.

Being gone for a week gave them time to land and make a foothold. A nest has been started on top one of the ducts. Branches were woven in a careless circle, together with other scraps, a bent parasol, a laundry line. In Holland, they welcome storks to their straw rooftops and chimneys, it's considered good luck. Not so with The Leopold. I have a broom to shoo them off.

When I'm around it's not a problem. They see me and that's generally enough, they'll give me a swoop as if to confide they've got their eye on me. There are other places for them to roost like the smokestacks of the shut factory or the armory on Jupiter Hill where there's a colony. All it takes is for me to be elsewhere and they'd make themselves a fine home. The Leopold is a perfect gliding path to the bay, for a beak full of fish, and the drafts swirl them efficiently right to the roof.

Mindful of the blue sky around me, I approached the nest. What would I do if there were already eggs in there? The manager would have a fit. I imagined lugging two cantaloupe heavy eggs down the ladder and the elevator, through the lobby to the front seat of the Nash. With the parents circling me as I drove to Tic Toc Travel. Could they be sent back to the Cretaceous? Frankly, it seems to me they've unlocked all kinds of problems opening these doors to the past.

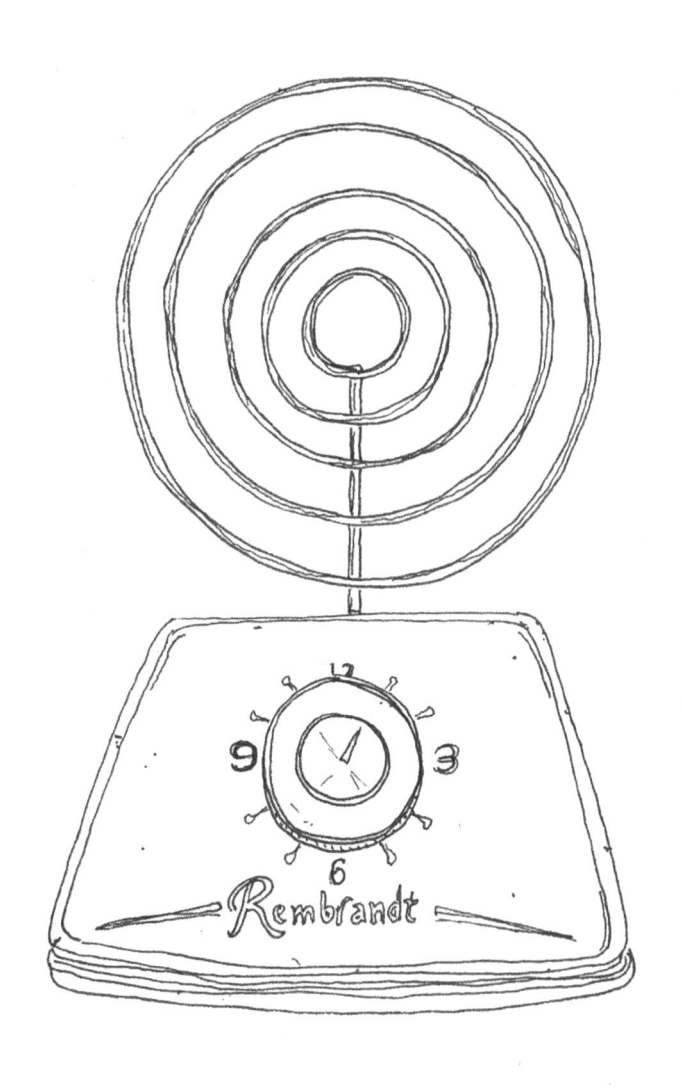

I checked the sky

THIS DAY and AGE

"Oh gee…" The pterodactyl nest wasn't my biggest problem, one of the flying lizards had crashed into a TV antenna. It lay tangled in black wire, broken tines and a bent over pole. It came a hundred million years just to crash into electricity. I think it was dead.

I checked the sky again before I took another step. I didn't want to be jumped by one of its friends while I examined it. It wasn't breathing. It was like a leather coat someone dropped, except for the claws and sharp teeth. The world's angriest leather jacket. When I turned its wing over with my shoe, a white sewn label showed. It wasn't Brooks Brothers, the words on the tag told me what to do:

IF FOUND, CONTACT TIC TOC TRAVEL

I pressed the red button next to the exposed wires that ran underneath its skin.

This wasn't a real prehistoric bird. It was a machine. Even so, I was close as I dared to be. I left it where it was. I had a nest to take apart. I want to keep my job and my rent-free tent and my Gamelan radio.

So I pulled the nest down and broke it apart. It's weird that Tic Toc would go to the trouble of programming a mechanical dinosaur to fly up here and build a nest, but a sewing machine has a job to do too. The nest was no well stitched textile though, apparently quality wasn't their company's concern.

It didn't take Tic Toc long to arrive, whirring in two chariots, settling down on the roof in a propwash making all the garden leaves lay flat. The rabbits were hiding, burrowed into the building's insulation tunneled out of sight. They were playing it smart, biding their time to fly, just a few hundred years of evolution lay ahead.

A crew wearing goggles and flight uniforms left their ships and quickly surrounded their malfunctioning creature. It took three of them to fold it like a napkin and carry it. "Don't worry," a woman assured me as they lifted it past me. "It'll be okay, it's just unconscious."

Sure. Sure it is…Possibly. It certainly seemed real. All I saw were some frayed wires—what if the pterodactyl had a pacemaker? A heart that old would be challenged beating in this day and age. I watched them heave the beast into a chariot. I shut my eyes and turned my head as the engines whined and the dust began to fly. Their departure scattered a nest jigsaw puzzle across the black crackling tar. It took me ten minutes to gather the pieces.

HAPPY WEDNESDAY

My Monday flower needed water. In fact it needed replanting in a valley full of other daisies like it, a long way from calendars. I commiserated. So far Monday had been difficult. If only Laika knew how soon we wilted. In her defense, I'm sure she would say you can't blame Monday—a Tuesday or Thursday could bring misfortune too. Yeah, I know. A Mondayist will cling to hope even if statistics say otherwise. There was nothing wrong with her enthusiasm though, and I like getting a flower. It does make the day better. Maybe the movement will spread throughout the week. A Wednesdayist might greet you with a chocolate. Why not? In a couple days I'll return to the B Minus Gallery and try that out on her.

I dipped the flower into one of the Gamalan teacups. It was a good size for it. I left the stem in the rainwater with the petals on the rim. For a second I thought I saw another bee, but it was only a ripple.

That made me think of Beckett. I hope he's enjoying the ocean. That's a lot of water to get lost in. I could stop by the Herald building, it was only two blocks away, and place a Lost Seal classified ad. Tomorrow morning or the next, a lighthouse keeper could be reading the newspaper, past the sports and the comics, tossing a sardine to his new pet on the floor now and then, turning the pages when he spots it: *Seal lost Monday*, with as much other detail as I could provide for the pocketful of money I carry. I stared across the city below. Beckett is out there somewhere, in a lighthouse, or in the sparkling bay.

Okay. There wasn't much more for me to do on the roof. It was pterodactyl free—the sky was too—not even a raincloud.

A rabbit ventured from the garden. What did it want?

"Don't look at me," I said. "I just work here."

my destination

TIME TAKES CARE of EVERYTHING

On the busy corner of Chestnut Street and Railroad Avenue people who have other places to go don't stop for long. My destination was the parking lot where I left the Nash but I waited for the red traffic light to change. My mind was still on pterodactyls, that's why when I saw the kiosk I thought there was enough room for a pterodactyl to stand in there, poised like someone in a phone booth. A dinosaur holding a quarter in a claw making an important call. Breathing uneasily. Are they all wired with makeshift hearts?

The traffic light turned green and I crossed the road and I read the words stitched to the black curtain that cloaked the booth: KNOW YOUR FUTURE. I couldn't resist those words, that curtain, those sequin stars. Everyone ought to know their future, I was surprised there wasn't a line a block long.

"Hello?" I couldn't see a break in the cloth. I don't know who went in and out of there. It was one continuous bolt of cloth, no beginning, no end. "Hello?"

"You want to know your future?" a woman said. She was hidden under the cloak of it, whoever she was, a voice wrapped in black typewriter ribbon.

"I wouldn't mind," I said.

"What do you do?" she asked.

What a question. I took a moment to examine the day so far. I told her I lose seals then look for them. I'm a sea urchin forgetter, avocado implanter, rain-loving daisy-dreaming traveler in time. And that's just today. So far.

"Why can't you say you're an artist?"

I laughed. Well, I don't know about that word. You might as well say unicorn.

Then it was her turn to laugh. "Do you know what's going to happen to you?"

Of course I don't. That's what made me stop here. I know something is going to happen. Will it be good? I hope so. I just don't know if it will be in time. It better happen soon. I'm starting to feel the breath of every precious day leaving me. Are there cures for electronic empires, will there be food on paper plates? The booth was silent. I listened to the city. Sonic revelations come to me. Dreamless nights bother me. Don't cross the picket line, don't be a ghost, you're alive right now. She didn't say anything else, but the message was clear: "Go find out."

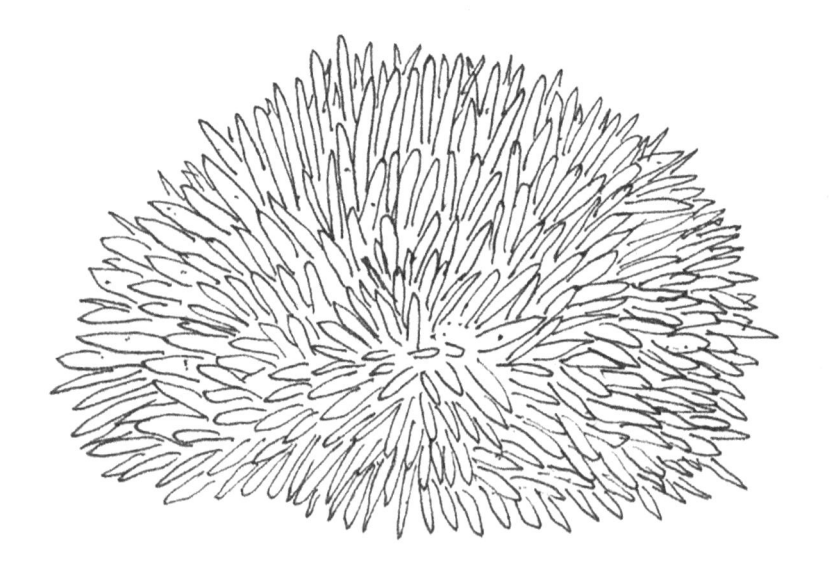

it's a wonder

HOLLY STREET HERO

The sea urchin slept on the front seat of the car in a see-through bag. It's a wonder those spines didn't pop the bubble. It could've driven the car down Holly Street, off the bridge into the safety of a saltwater creek. The Nash pushed deep in the mud with a trickle of low tide going round, periwinkles, eelgrass, plover. What a story that sea urchin would tell when it rejoined the scuttling crowds in the ocean shallows, speaking on a barnacle stone in a beam of wavering green sunlight. What a hero.

I started the car and steered. I pictured calling Gloria about the fate of her beautiful Nash if that episode occurred. A wheezing crane on the overpass winching it free. That disaster together with Beckett's disappearance would really hurt my chances of ever housesitting again. A street later when the telephone under the dashboard rang, I had a feeling it was her, checking up on me.

Gloria sounded happy, giddy actually, caught up in the elation that surrounded being a movie star. She told me she was staying an extra day or two for more promotion. She was dining with the prince of Tahiti. That's fine with me I said, she can stay in France as long as she wants, I don't mind. It gives me a little more time to find that missing seal.

"How are you and Beckett getting along?" she asked.

"Oh, fine," I lied.

"Can I speak with him?"

"Not right now, I'm in the car. He's at home sleeping." Truth, lie, truth, lie, it was like being on *Where'd It Go?* And like that show I wouldn't be able to keep it up for long. I didn't want her to worry, not when she was thousands of miles from here and there was nothing she could do. Who am I kidding? If she knew Beckett went astray, she'd have the Coast Guard combing every fathom. Billboards would patch the city walls and stilt the skyline and she'd be on TV offering a reward. What a tearful commercial that would be, sad seal eyes and music to match. I didn't want it to come to that, not while I still have a little extra time and a chance of finding that misplaced animal. I believe in my ability.

WHAT COMES BACK

This town is full of mysteries, you can't go down the street without running into a detective. Some of them I'm acquainted with. I saw Jones Jr. kneeled beside a red bicycle tire. Denton Pines, Howard Plaid. I could stop the car and count them amble by, but I haven't considered hiring one, not really, until I spotted Charlie Chan in his white suit with his wife and thirteen children in tow. If anyone could find Beckett, he could, but his mind ticks at a much higher altitude, solving crime in realms of espionage and intrigue, poisons and smoking guns, wax museums, circuses, steamships, creaking houses in the dark. A seal is just a vapor swimming past. I gave the Nash some gas and weaved between the streetcars and trolleys.

The sea urchin bag wobbled on the next turn. I promised as soon as we were home, we'd go to the beach and get a bucket of fresh cold seawater. Peckinpaw's gave me directions: "float the unopened bag for fifteen minutes to acclimate your pet to its new environment. Then, open the bag and slowly add water by hand or cup until ready for release."

The same directions apply to me. When the sun goes down and I get to the beach, I need to decompress from my travels in town. I sit on the sand and dig my fingers in and I become still. "For fifteen minutes allow yourself to adjust to your new world." That's been my practice every night this week. After a day like today I can use it. The surf erases and redraws. Calming down, with my eyes shut, the water takes my jumbled thoughts and strings them out like clothes on a laundry line, going, going, some of them dragging the tops of swells, some of them pulled deep through the current, until finally I can think of one thing. All that's left on the line is a rabbit. I let it go like a kite into sky or a radio message sent far into the airwaves. When it's gone, there's nothing left of me.

I lowered the visor, chrome blinked, the engine growled at the sunshine, we were leaving town in a honey jar, trees and windows pointed at the sea.

What am I thinking about? The bucket I will bring to the beach. My fingers in the sand. The water calling me. All we have are thoughts.

Whatever I want to give, I can put in a bucket. A pterodactyl thought, a gamelan note? Something the sea never saw. I toss it out. The water takes that and sends me something in trade. I pull on the rope tied to the handle. Turning around and reeled back in, returning with something heavy, flashing silver, zigzagging back and forth. About to emerge from the sea. Whatever I project comes back to me.

The Nash slowed, I pressed a button on the dashboard and the gate opened and we were at Gloria's. Time flies when you're having fun

CHAMPION of MY IMAGINARY GAMESHOW

A white clam shell was left tipped against the door. My first thought was: is this an art project? Will I step into a room full of seawater? Starfish on the walls, a school of herring, kelp winding up from the floor, breathing out bubbles. I bent and picked up the smooth shell and read what was written on it: "Seal in boat." This was the sort of clue that would set off the music in a movie—I swear I think I heard it as I ran around the house on the flagstones that melted into sand that turned into dunes and the stereo of water meeting land.

The rowboat was where I left it. I let go of the sea urchin bag when I saw Beckett asleep inside the hull. What did he care about the day he put me through? The sun was slowly setting on a long day at sea. "Seal in boat," I laughed. Mortality has no meaning—when you see someone you thought was gone forever, you know that's true. I jumped around like Ben Gunn, but Beckett showed little reaction. He opened one eye and shut it again. The harness remained on him, with a few feet of line still attached.

"How are you?" I asked. No response. Beckett was tired. Swimming for ten hours will do that. "Well, it's good to see you, pal," I said a little quieter. I was tired too. I got a chair out of the tall beachgrass and set it next to the rowboat. I sat down. I bet I could fall asleep in 53 seconds—there's another gameshow I could master—*Fast Asleep*—who will be first?

Before I shut my eyes, I remembered the shell. I took it out of my pocket, along with a pen. I try to always have a pen and paper with me. I wrote a reply on the shell underneath the previous message. THANKS. I leaned over and placed it against the boat. Whoever directed me here would see it. The judge on *Fast Asleep* set the clock as I got comfortable again, prepared after years of training for the competition, ready to wake up to applause, a trophy, the live studio band. But as my eyes began to shut, a last look at the beach, my urge to sleep stalled.

I don't know why I felt I had to examine them, hundreds of prints are left in the sand every day, I guess a part of me was remembering Charlie Chan. Never overlook a clue. Close as I was to being champion of my imaginary gameshow, I got to my feet to investigate.

Walking beside the footprints, I guessed the person was a little smaller than me, the pacing of the steps was less far apart. They crossed a trail of bird feet arrows, sand dollars and broken shells, and then a place where a bird made a paintbrushed landing imprinting weight in the sand. Nothing was that strange until I got close to the incoming tide. It caught me off guard, it almost reached my shoes. The waves ran up fast along the sand and the footprints disappeared suddenly in the hiss.

miracles occur

COMPARED with the OCEAN

I woke up looking at the night sky. Stars and planets. Everything you see out there happened in the past. Old news. Million-year-old dots of light scattered on the sea. Similarly, across the water miles from me, time in Honolulu is three hours behind. Different time zones. The sun that was here is back there, shining. I don't know what that means exactly, I can't tell them anything about the future: racehorses cross finish lines, kings and queens are crowned, disasters and miracles occur, but wherever you are everything is happening at the same moment. Clocks and calendars don't exist.

I yawned and listened. A big radio tuned to the ocean. Some nights I can find this same wavelength on the Leopold roof above the rushing sigh of the city.

Maybe I ought to go back to the house. It was late, I wasn't all that comfortable sleeping in a chair. For one thing, my shoes are wet—no wonder—the water washed around my feet. It was hightide. Very. I stopped daydreaming about time and left my aluminum chair, grabbing it before it could float away.

A seal face yawned in the rowboat. Still giving me the cold shoulder. For some reason I thought Beckett would be happier to see me. I'm just the guy who allows a roof overhead, refills a food bowl and a plastic swimming pool. I can't compare with the ocean.

I took the end of Beckett's rope and I said, "Let's go home."

Beckett groaned, but he slopped over the hull and splashed.

It's unusual for the tide to come this far. Good thing the rowboat was anchored in the beachgrass or it surely would have gone looking for Hawaii. That urchin from Peckinpaw's did. I dropped the bag on the sand when I came here. I didn't mean to forget. The tide knew what to do with it. Aloha, sea urchin.

Beckett made quite a racket clapping those

flippers in the shallow water. Nobody heard us though, the houses by the sea were dark. Their seals were already tucked in for the night, curled in wading pools in living rooms with million-dollar paintings by Marc Chagall.

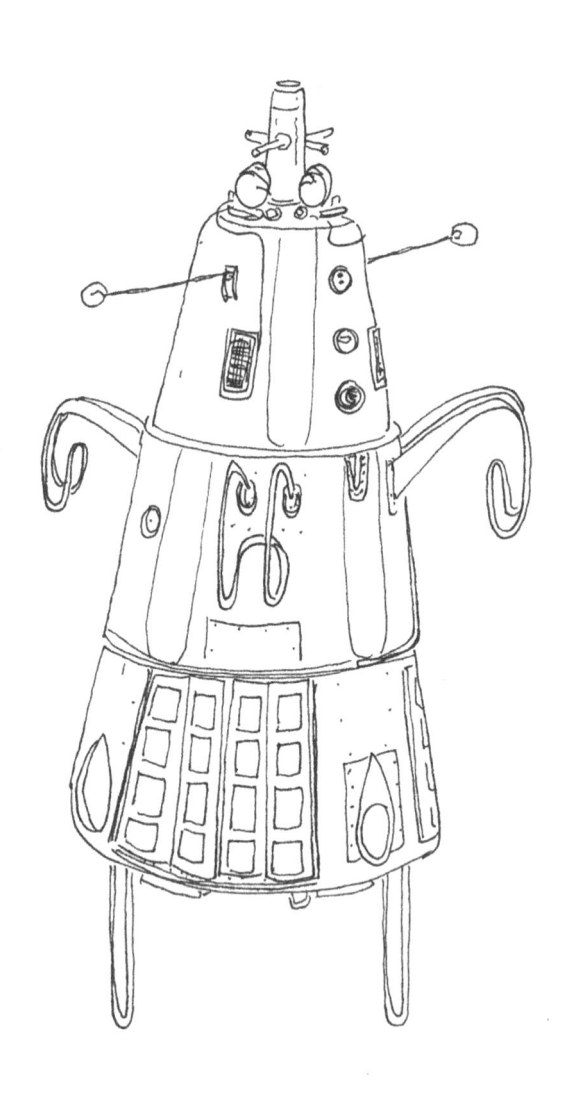

maybe you'll find one

The GALLERY CALLS

When I worked at the factory I used to do a little subtle sabotage. Just to make things interesting. Remember, we were stamping out houses on an assembly line, each one was the same, there shouldn't be any deviation, if you went to the moon or found yourself on some habitable meteor, you were supposed to find the same America waiting for you. I never liked that idea. I want to walk around a corner and be surprised by a medieval steeple or go under elm trees guarding the street. There should be no end to the possibilities. So I wrote messages. Maybe you'll find one someday on Saturn or who knows where—if I happen to find myself in one of the colonies, I will look. I couldn't make it real obvious, my work has to go under the radar. I never expect to see those words again, they're a surprise for whoever finds them.

The window curtain breeze transported birdsongs and stuck them on the walls. I tracked how they moved right up to the vaulted ceiling. From the light in my bedroom, I guessed it was around eight. The birds start singing around four o'clock when it's still dark and I'm cradled around the room by them until I fall back asleep.

Not today though—the phone started to clatter. People can make sounds like Thelonious Monk, I would have preferred that. Still, when a telephone rings it could be important news. I left the bed and the birds, and I reached for the phone on the bedside table.

It was Laika. She was pretty excited. "You better come to the gallery right away!" She sounded like someone trying with difficulty not to run from a rhinoceros. What could be that bad about a room called The Same as Yesterday.

"Is it about the review in the *Herald*?" I asked.

She sighed and repeated what she already said. I told her I'd be there soon.

Gloria's house knows when its occupant is awake. I heard the coffee machine gurgling in the kitchen automatically. I got dressed.

The birds were going too. They're not actually

stuck on the walls, that's my imagination, they don't need a gallery, they're in the world everywhere.

AMELIA EARHART

Amelia Earhart was searching the gray sidewalk, walking slowly, trying to find something that must have been small as an innertube lost in the Pacific. I don't think she noticed me, her eyes were binoculars intent on little things. Solo flying. I didn't have time to help, sorry, the B Minus was just ahead. Laika made me think the worst, that the gallery doors would be broken open and roosting with a pelican invasion, but it looked like an ordinary morning to me. The hanging flower baskets were still draining after being watered, pattering the cement underneath. A sparrow fluttered in the drops.

When I got to the doorway, I almost turned around. Being with Amelia Earhart was better than what was waiting in the gallery. Oh gee, not him...Laika was listening to my clone.

I'll admit, my fleeting aspirations may not all

be good, and my flesh and blood may not become something made of statue tin. It was a bad idea getting myself cloned—that was a year ago, I thought it would be an interesting art performance. Live and learn.

Morris Oscar was my nemesis.

He knew I was near. He turned around and announced me, "Oscar Morris! And this is your show, is it?"

"Hi Morris," I said.

"I read about this…" he pointed at the empty room. Not so empty now, it echoed with his nasal bray. I don't sound like that. At least I hope I don't. "The Same as Yesterday, huh?"

"That's right." What was he up to?

"There's just one problem, Oscar." He paused and I saw Laika on the other side of him, trying with difficulty not to run from a rhinoceros. "This is *my* idea."

"What?"

He waved a postcard at me.

"What is it?" I asked.

"Look."

Reluctantly I joined them.

"This is *my* show," he said and handed me the

card. "Look familiar?"

"Morris Oscar," I read the bold print. Below was a solemn photograph of him. I read the next letters even bolder, "Antifluxus..." I asked, "Antifluxus? What's that?"

I heard Laika gulp.

"Keep reading," he said.

I read the smaller print, "The Past is Today. Now showing at the Yvette DerGleritsch Museum of Fine Art." It opened last week.

Morris glared at me. His face was pinched as a wooden mask.

I asked Laika, "Why can't I get a card like this?" When my show opened, it was announced on a few photocopies stapled to telephone poles.

"I want this stopped," he gritted. People have said we look alike, but I disagree. "If my demand isn't met, your gallery will be shut down in..." he glanced at his watch—I don't wear one of those either—"I'll give you one hour."

Laika tried to say something about how we had no idea.

"Don't you read the *Herald*?" He had one in his valise. I recognized the frontpage from last week. The headlines were already old news. He poked at the feature article. I looked away.

I never saw it. I don't read the newspaper, I leave that to Laika.

Her eyes were shut.

"One hour!" Morris boomed. My clone spun on his leather boots so his long coat whirled like a cape.

CONDEMNED

"I'm sorry," Laika said, "I forgot to mention that article. We were so busy with the install and promotion. I just assumed you and Morris were joining forces on your shows."

"No, not at all. He's my curse. I wish I never created him."

"Well, his article was really something—front page—it's a glowing review. He's really gaining footing as an artist."

"Okay, Laika."

"Your show is great too. But his got noticed." She held up her hands dramatically and recited, "'Take a breath and step inside a stillness that stays the same.' I memorized that line."

"Laika!"

She shrunk, "Sorry."

I don't want to be her rhinoceros, but Morris Oscar made me one.

"What should we do?" she said.

"Nothing."

"Nothing?"

I nodded.

"But they'll shut us down. Morris said so!"

"This is a two-week show, we can't change it, it has to stay the same, it's in the title."

Laika clutched her fingers together.

I said, "You don't have to do anything to it." I gave her a smile. It was supposed to be pleasant. Maybe it didn't work.

"What if he comes back with the law?"

I worked that smile again. "Don't worry, Laika."

She tried. When she was back at her desk holding a book, I left.

Two hours later when I happened to return, there was newspaper taped all over the gallery windows. A white sign with red and black lettering was tacked on the door: CLOSED. Condemned. Do Not Enter.

GHOST DIRECTIONS

I left the B Minus, the Nash was on the next block, not far from where Amelia Earhart had traveled to. She was still hunting for something. I thought I could help. As I walked, I began looking too and I don't even know what I'm looking for! When I spotted a penny, I picked it up. I had two barrettes and another penny by the time I reached her. The Nash was parked nearby.

I said, "Excuse me. Can I help?"

She was startled by my question. The goggles on top her head glinted with sunshine.

"You're Amelia Earhart, right?"

"Yes," she quickly agreed.

"Did you lose something?"

"Yes." She kept walking, "I can't say what it is." She stopped at a garbage can and examined its contents.

Okay, I'm not going to cause trouble. I'm not like Morris. Just the thought of him and my pace increased. He was a scoundrel, especially since he decided he was an artist too. One time Morris offered to buy an idea from me. I needed rent, this was before the Leopold, and I mean if I didn't come up with the money, I was on the street, so I gave him Ghosts in the Gallery. I would have done that show myself, I should have, but I'll admit I was scared of installing ghosts in the floor. When it was a hit, he got the credit, and he was more than happy taking that.

I poured the barrettes and pennies off my hand onto the sidewalk. If that's what she was looking for, she would find them when she got here. I arrived at the car and got the key from my pocket. Where now, Nash Statesman 600? A piece of paper was bent between the front wheel and the curb. I'm not the sort to ignore a clue, not even one in the gutter. I unfolded the paper and turned it over to read the side that was written on:

DIRECTIONS for being Amelia Earhart. You were born in Kansas on July 24, 1897. You are a famous pilot. Your nickname is Queen of the Air. You are the first woman to cross the Atlantic Ocean alone. You disappeared in 1937 trying to fly around the world. You are an inspiration.

Other paragraphs listed things to mention, events of her day, how to make casual conversation with the people of this century. The letterhead was the Tic Toc Travel logo. At the bottom, the red letters warned: *Do Not Lose or Reveal This Document. Penalties Apply.*

I looked at the way I'd come. Amelia Earhart was making her stealthy way. I had a feeling she was looking for this. Did she forget who she was? I returned to her and asked, "Are you looking for this?"

Her reaction to this litter was pure joy, as if what I showed her was the way off the ocean to an unclouded runway in Oakland, California.

A RAINY-DAY SONG

I drove back towards Gloria's, past the landmarks I've grown accustomed to, haloed by the first pterodactyl catching breeze. Beckett needs his morning swim. I turned the radio on, no rainy songs today. A sunny blue sky. After yesterday's adventure with Beckett in the ocean, I decided we'd go to the seal park instead. In a way it's easier. He can't disappear. I don't need a boat or all the gear. No spool of line running off into the unknown depths. But the seal park is a whole other scene.

One morning it was raining and I didn't feel like rowing so we piled in the car and off we went. A tourist bus was stopped in front of the gate, I remember I had to wait. Staring through the metal bars. The Nash with windshield wipers going like a tiger washing its face. The guide must have been telling them who lived here. I saw people at the windows rub the glass. I suppose they thought I was driving Gloria, they might have seen the seal blur in the backseat and chirped, "There she is!" Then the bus was on to the next star's house. We might as well have been rowing, I could have been driving a submarine through all the water between home and the seal park. I braked beside a guardhouse before a red and white boom gate and rolled my window down. Not just anyone can enter, it's members only, so I showed Gloria's card. He nodded and the gate raised. Beckett started to bark. He kept that up until we parked. It *is* exciting, I'll admit. The building looks like a Roman temple, columns, statues, a fountain in front and inside is an enormous blue water swimming pool filled with seals. They love it. They chase each other and leap off slides, in and out while we wander around the poolside, chauffeurs, nannies, millionaires, or we sit in the marble stands and watch. The last time I was there I saw Esther Williams.

    An open-air tour bus painted like a toy chattered beneath an orange tree. There were so many mansions to see and maybe someone famous like Don Ameche walking a seal. Would I miss all this when Gloria returned? When I was living in the elements in the sky, keeping the dinosaurs away.

I turned the radio dial. Sometimes you want to hear a rainy-day song.

ANOTHER SEASHELL

Another seashell. And here I go again. I lifted it up and read the other curved side of it: "Seal With Me." What? I tried the house door—it was open, did I leave it that way? Possibly. When I was in a hurry to get to the gallery, no time for coffee, no idea why Laika was calling me. I hurried across the cool tiles in the hall to where I could see the wading pool by the window. It was empty, no seal. "Beckett!" Not on the couches, not in the other rooms, not up the stairs on the other floors. "Beckett!" Oh, come on—first they find Beckett, then they take him away? I was right back at yesterday.

I opened the sliding glass door and went onto the deck. Beckett likes it out here, he sticks his head between the rails like a prisoner watching the sea. A rubber beach ball in the corner by a chair. Who knew having a seal was such an unforgiving chore—maybe I was just bad at it.

A sailboat drifted origami slow, far offshore. The other rowboats weren't out yet, it was a lazy day for some people. Short waves shuffled. A couple snow white clouds.

Last night's hightide swept the sand clean around our moored boat. Footprints walked past it to the house and returned to the water with Beckett's flopping wake beside them. Who was coming and going from the sea?

On my way down the steps, I grabbed a big cone. It looks like I'm holding a Rudy Vallee megaphone, good for crooning at people on the sand, but it has another use too. There's air and there's water and sound carries in both.

Following Beckett's path, I stopped before the sand got wet to take off my shoes and socks. That involved a bit of balancing, standing on one leg like a heron. Gracefully? Not quite. Then I rolled my pants up to my knees. Whoever walked before me didn't bother with that procedure, their bare feet led Beckett right into the sea. It was cold too. I had to stand in the shallow and get numb. It felt like I was laced into ice wingtips. I had to make friends with the water, like petting a polar bear.

Once I was far enough in, I dipped the horn into the water and called into it, "Beckett!" I might be the only one in the world to ever do this. If only it worked.

Where were they? Were they submerged beyond the reach of daylight? Were they reined to cormorants skimming down the coast? Those birds are a common sight around here, going from one harbor to another. I doubt they're pulling seals though.

I called "Beckett" a little weaker one last time. It wasn't working. So much for Rudy Vallee. Well...what if Beckett was answering me? With the horn pressed in the water, I held my ear to the mouthpiece and listened, the way a kid would listen to a shell. The locomotive surge of the ocean functioning, a kind of vinyl scratching tone, and small as one faucet left dripping in a railyard rooming house, my own heartbeat.

The MAGIC PLANET

Maybe I give up too easily, maybe that's my problem in so many ways, but after only hearing my heart, I left the beach. I could have heaved the boat into the water and called all day and rang the bell and seen nothing through the telescope but a fish or two if I was lucky. Whoever borrowed Beckett seemed to be taking care of him. All I needed was a shell to know he was doing alright.

I surveyed the ocean from the deck. Not much had changed, the clouds had changed shape, the sailboat was a little further. If I had the telescope I'd see if Beckett was on the boat. This is a magic planet, anything can happen at any time to throw you for a loop, you never know what will happen next. For instance, this:

Someone was knocking at the front door. Gloria doesn't get unannounced visitors. The gate sees to that. Unless I left it open when I got back. I must have. There's a lot on my mind. I opened the door and a man in a black chauffeur's suit tapped his hat.

He said, "Excuse me, sir."

"Yes?"

"Pardon the intrusion but my employer sent me here to ask if you may have seen our seal." He showed me a photo. It was a seal wearing a captain's braided cap. "This is Renwick."

"Oh gee. Your seal is missing too?"

The chauffeur explained that apparently there was an epidemic all along the seafront. Seal rustlers? There—see, I didn't expect that. We didn't have long to talk, he gave me a card, he had more houses to go to, and Gloria's telephone was ringing in the hall.

"I better get that," I told him. A seal syndicate? I didn't get that impression. Those seashells didn't feel like ransom notes. I truly expect Beckett to be returned. This might even be a call from that sailboat, ship to shore, inviting me to join them.

I picked up the phone and said hello.

It was Laika. "Your clone is here with the police."

"Oh brother." Leave it to Morris to turn a quiet

room into a crime scene. I was my own worst enemy.

"Can you come back?"

"I was just there, Laika."

"They're terminating the show."

"Isn't that illegal? Tell him we have a contract. Isn't it ironclad, can't a gallery show what they want?"

"It's borderline. He says it's infringing on his creative property. I don't want to go to jail over this, Oscar."

"I understand. I'll be there soon." What I don't understand is people like Morris who think they can take credit for the inspiration this planet willingly gives us all.

MORE than a DIME

Two things slowed me down. Two bus stops, to be precise.

Remember I said this town is full of detectives? Phil Ticks is the original gumshoe detective. He sat on a bus stop bench with a leg on his knee, picking at his sole with an apartment key. He really did have gum on his shoe. I had to smile. I drove close to the curb and stopped. I rolled the window down and called out, "Hey Phil! What's new?"

He shrugged.

"Say, I might have a job for you." I told him about the seals. I dug out the card Renwick's butler gave me. "You should give him a call. There's probably a reward."

"I'd like to, but I'm already employed."

I noticed the butterfly net on the bench next to him and asked him about it.

"Yeah," he nodded, "I need to find a lost moth. Talk about a needle in a haystack."

I wanted to know more about it, but a bus horn bleated behind me and hissed its brakes. The Nash was parked in its spot. I waved at Phil and stepped on the gas. Seals and moths are going missing. I can't figure it. Are they related? The ocean is wide and deep and so is the city's atmosphere. A seal, a moth, what's the difference if they're gone and someone misses them. I've got enough fuss with my seal, I'm just glad it isn't my job to wave a net at every neon sign in town. Poor Phil. I let the steering wheel run through my hands as I left Belmont Street.

I tried to imagine why someone would hire a private investigator to find a moth. What for? Was something written on the wings? A safe combination?

Thoughts of moths summoned another lost flier, but this time I looked for a legal spot to park. I put a dime in the meter. Amelia Earhart was at a bus stop a hundred feet away from me when I started towards her. There's something I've been thinking about that I just can't resolve. That paper I found in the gutter. She remembered me—she didn't need reminding—then why did she need directions for herself?

"I'm not really Amelia Earhart," she revealed. "Tic Toc hires actors. My last gig was a walk-on role in *Our Town*. I thought this would help my career. Forget it. It's not for me." She looked past me, down the street, "I'm quitting."

"Hold on. Wait a minute. There's no time travel?"

"It's a masquerade. We just play the parts. People see us, they talk to us, they think time travel is possible then they go to Tic Toc and pay a fortune to try it themselves. Have you been there, have you tried it?"

"No." I don't have a fortune. I live on a roof.

"There's a big room with a spiraling circle on the wall. It spins and hypnotizes you. For an hour you're just lost somewhere in your mind. When they pull you out, you think you've been to a place that no longer exists. You might as well be asleep in a dream."

I needed more than a dime in the meter for this.

WHERE WE ARE

I offered Amelia Earhart a ride to the time travel agency. Sorry—I know she isn't that famous aviator, but I never got her real name. Besides, she looked like Amelia. She just didn't want to be her anymore. I couldn't believe the story she was telling me. Tic Toc was a hoax! What happens when the word gets out?

Traffic slowed on Prospect Street. "Woah!" I said, "What's going on?"

A celebrity crowd holding signs marched on the sidewalk. They were picketing Tic Toc Travel. I read some signs as I braked, "On Strike, Time Travel Unfair, Get Real Tic Toc."

Amelia laughed, "Look at this! I'm not the only one!"

Salvador Dali waved a giant cardboard clock. We were stopped. They were chanting, "Time to change! Time to change!" as Amelia hopped out the door. Cars on the street were honking horns, we edged forward. I lost Amelia in the crowd. It was something to see, all those people from history protesting the future.

Newsflash—we can't go back and forth in time, all those marchers on Prospect were ordinary like me, Amelia Earhart doesn't exist. Yesterday is done, I can't even hold it still in the controlled environment of The B Minus Gallery. I turned at the next corner, en route to my next stop.

It's a concept we need to accept. What's wrong with where we are now? And can't we work together to make our time better? I'm grateful for where I am, here on Earth at this moment.

Almost, that is...There was newspaper taped all over the gallery windows. A white sign with red and black lettering was tacked on the door: CLOSED. Condemned. Do Not Enter.

I parked. He did it. Morris Oscar strikes again. I was walking faster than usual. My shadow scribbled along the concrete. It poured into one splotch as I stopped. I couldn't see through the *Herald* pages stuck in a curtain inside the windows, but one of the articles caught my attention: "AREA MAN ASLEEP IN THE HAY. Sam—" the last name was hidden under brown tape "—has long denied that he's been sleeping in a haystack. Yet coworkers admit he's been showing up to work with bits of hay in his hair, and occasionally a tiny feather stuck to his suit." A gray photograph of him sleeping in a haystack accompanied the story. Mother Goose would be proud of him. I tried the gallery door. It was locked.

I knocked and called Laika's name. While I waited, the CLOSED sign stared at me like an evil window. To anyone passing by, The B Minus Gallery was a wanted poster in a post office. You needed to know the story. *Age: 68. Height: 2 stories. Build: Brick, yellow pine, terracotta. Occupation: Gallery. Scars and Marks: Crumbled masonry, bees on second floor, graffiti on alley side.* And what was the criminal record? Did the gallery hold up a 7-Eleven in Burien and get away with cash and five cartons of Hope cigarettes? No, this was all because of Morris Oscar.

The GIFT

These were the days when an older America was still on the air, when you could see The Jackson 5 and *The Outer Limits* on rerun. Watching TV is seeing different Americas. When night falls, after Mary Tyler Moore meows, used car commercials, Count Misfit runs old movies with Bela Lugosi, castles, swamps, galaxies. The Count commissioned me to paint their backdrop, a dark forest and stars. So in a way I continue to be on TV. It's like having gallery space in Transylvania.

My shadow stopped again suddenly at Admiral Television Repair. Five TVs in the display window showed the same familiar scene. Familiar to me. A gameshow set. A shimmering video repeat of *Where'd It Go?* I froze. It was me on all five screens. My ghost from the past haunting me. Three cards were dealt before me. This was week two on the show when I was unbeatable. Everyone was rooting for me or waiting for me to stumble. No sound came through the thick glass as I answered correctly and the camera turned to the applauding audience. There must be millions of hours of programs that are cataloged from the gray beginnings of TV history to now, why play this? "Oh gee…" Look at that plaid suit I was wearing! I remember the day I got that off a Goodwill rack. My lucky plaid suit.

"You still got the gift?"

Someone was behind me. Gift? No, my plaid suit was long gone.

He repeated, "I said you still got the gift?"

The guy looked like he spent his spare time bending lampposts. I said, "You mean gift for cards?

"That's right."

"Oh gee, I don't know. I haven't touched them since then." When I wore a plaid suit.

"Let's see if you're still any good." He gripped my arm and we turned from the window. I didn't resist, I already knew what he did with lampposts.

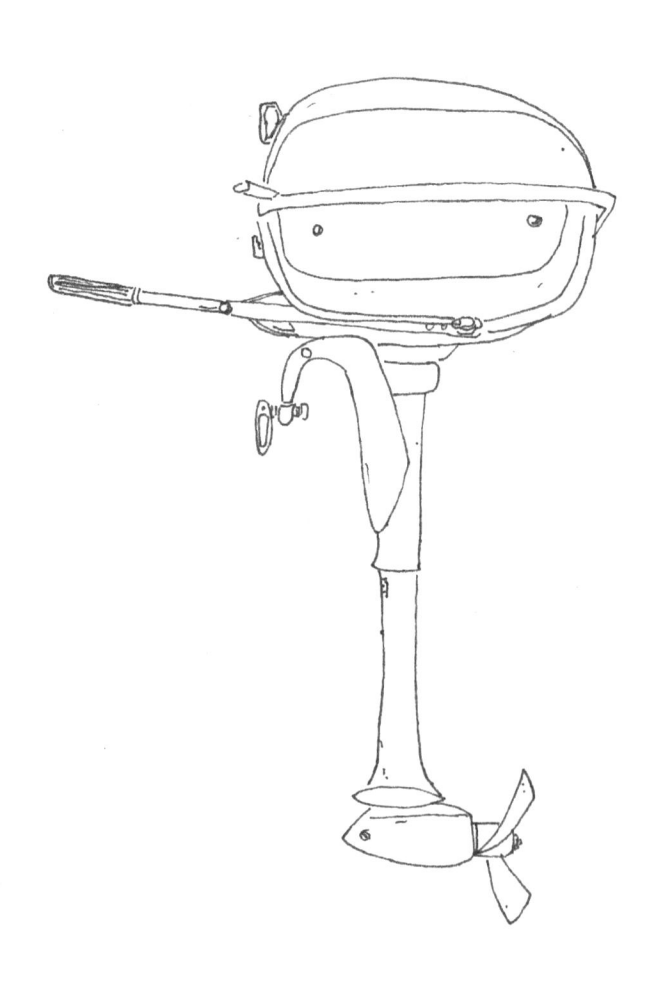

getting it started

MERCY

This was no Nash Statesman 600. We were on a motorboat, an old wooden cabin cruiser like the one in *To Have and Have Not*. It was stolen. There's a story there, but I won't go into it. I can't deny I had a part in it. I stood watch on the dock while he tinkered with the boat, finally getting it started. It was nighttime, after a long day of guessing cards in a waterfront fish shack and hours spent going over a plan that seemed doomed to fail. The ocean was chopping around us. My brain was rattled. All I got to eat was a can of artificial avocado and each bouncing wave was determined to get it back.

My captor never told me his name. Good idea. If I got out of this, I could turn him in for all manner of crimes, not least of which is culinary. This was his plan:

The Clepsydra drifted in the blackness ahead, just outside of international waters. She's a gambling ship. It was his bright idea to use me to break the bank. He even brought along a disguise for me, a beard that looks like it fell off a yak. This guy thought of everything.

He thought of everything except gas.

The engine sputtered, coughed and stopped. The propeller locked. We hushed through the next swell and slowed to a drifting halt.

We were a long way offshore.

Floating.

Whoever-he-was left the wheel and stomped down the steps into the cabin area. The engine compartment was under the floorboards. I was drawn outside to the deck platform. It was cool and quiet. Just me and a zillion gallons of water. I sat on the siding. The wake had already been eaten by the waves. No sign of land or the gambling ship. I expected to see her dot of light like a star on the horizon and then as we got closer we'd hear the murmur of the band playing on deck. Not tonight, friend, we were at the mercy of the sea.

I thought of all the times this must have happened to those sailing ships that relied on the wind being there. We're at the mercy of larger things. Whirlpools and sargasso weeds and leviathans. Lifeboats, rafts, someone clinging to a torpedoed remain. I let go, I felt soothed, calmed by the petting surge, waiting for whatever had to happen. The streetlamp bender in the hull was making a lot of noise—if he wasn't, I could have been at one with the ocean, wobbled like a raindrop stuck on glass, not surprised when a cold wet hand reached up out of the water and wrapped around my arm and pulled me down.

MY TAXI

We spoke by seashell. I finally met the author, my seal's guardian angel. She had green hair, blue eyes, shiny chestnut skin. Swimming wasn't a problem for her. I was doing alright too. She put me on the back of a pilot whale, my taxi back to land.

I don't know how she learned to write. I didn't ask her if there were underwater schools. Plenty of books have gone down in ships, the ABCs begin with Anemone. She learned. She was able to go on land too, I've seen her footprints when she isn't wearing a tail. Maybe she listened at classroom windows, hidden by shadows or leaves. I'm sure there's more insight to be gained from talking to a mermaid, but I'm not much of a conversationist. We kept it simple. Besides, there's not much room for words on a seashell.

What did I ask her about? Did she make art?

She showed me her bracelet. Where did she live? She went with the water. She asked me about the rain. Do I like music? Does she like birds? Do I like fish? I asked if she ever saw movies. We just made small talk while the taxi whale carried me and she swam effortlessly. We were getting to know each other. I could see a glow and then the little shining eyes of houses in the night. We were getting near—I could smell the warm love of land. She asked me about the moon. I wrote it was in outer space, another world beyond this one. She looked up with watery eyes. I did too. The worlds go on and on and on and on.

7/12/2024
6:30 PM

FLOP

Writing: May—July 2024

from *The Tin Can Telephone* (2020)

Books by Good Deed Rain

Saint Lemonade, Allen Frost, 2014. Two novels illustrated by the author in the manner of the old Big Little Books.

Playground, Allen Frost, 2014. Poems collected from seven years of chapbooks.

Roosevelt, Allen Frost, 2015. A Pacific Northwest novel set in July, 1942, when a boy and a girl search for a missing elephant. Illustrated throughout by Fred Sodt.

5 Novels, Allen Frost, 2015. Novels written over five years, featuring circus giants, clockwork animals, detectives and time travelers.

The Sylvan Moore Show, Allen Frost, 2015. A short story omnibus of 193 stories written over 30 years.

Town in a Cloud, Allen Frost, 2015. A three part book of poetry, written during the Bellingham rainy seasons of fall, winter, and spring.

A Flutter of Birds Passing Through Heaven: A Tribute to Robert Sund, 2016. Edited by Allen Frost and Paul Piper. The story of a legendary Ish River poet & artist.

At the Edge of America, Allen Frost, 2016. Two novels in one book blend time travel in a mythical poetic America.

Lake Erie Submarine, Allen Frost, 2016. A two week vacation in Ohio inspired these poems, illustrated by the author.

and Light, Paul Piper, 2016. Poetry written over three years. Illustrated with watercolors by Penny Piper.

The Book of Ticks, Allen Frost, 2017. A giant collection of 8 mysterious adventures featuring Phil Ticks. Illustrated throughout by Aaron Gunderson.

I Can Only Imagine, Allen Frost, 2017. Five adventures of love and heartbreak dreamed in an imaginary world. Cover & color illustrations by Annabelle Barrett.

The Orphanage of Abandoned Teenagers, Allen Frost, 2017. A fictional guide for teens and their parents. Illustrated by the author.

In the Valley of Mystic Light: An Oral History of the Skagit Valley Arts Scene, 2017. A comprehensive illustrated tribute. Edited by Claire Swedberg & Rita Hupy.

Different Planet, Allen Frost, 2017. Four science fiction adventures: reincarnation, robots, talking animals, outer space and clones. Cover & illustrations by Laura Vasyutynska.

Go with the Flow: A Tribute to Clyde Sanborn, 2018. Edited by Allen Frost. The life and art of a timeless river poet. In beautiful living color!

Homeless Sutra, Allen Frost, 2018. Four stories: Sylvan Moore, a flying monk, a water salesman, and a guardian rabbit.

The Lake Walker, Allen Frost 2018. A little novel set in black and white like one of those old European movies about death and life.

A Hundred Dreams Ago, Allen Frost, 2018. A winter book of poetry and prose. Illustrated by Aaron Gunderson.

Almost Animals, Allen Frost, 2018. A collection of linked stories, thinking about what makes us animals.

The Robotic Age, Allen Frost, 2018. A vaudeville magician and his faithful robot track down ghosts. Illustrated throughout by Aaron Gunderson.

Kennedy, Allen Frost, 2018. This sequel to *Roosevelt* is a coming-of-age fable set during two weeks in 1962 in a mythical Kennedyland. Illustrated throughout by Fred Sodt.

Fable, Allen Frost, 2018. There's something going on in this country and I can best relate it in fable: the parable of the rabbits, a bedtime story, and the diary of our trip to Ohio.

Elbows & Knees: Essays & Plays, Allen Frost, 2018. A thrilling collection of writing about some of my favorite subjects, from B-movies to Brautigan.

The Last Paper Stars, Allen Frost 2019. A trip back in time to the 20 year old mind of Frankenstein, and two other worlds of the future.

Walt Amherst is Awake, Allen Frost, 2019. The dreamlife of an office worker. Illustrated throughout by Aaron Gunderson.

When You Smile You Let in Light, Allen Frost, 2019. An atomic love story written by a 23 year old.

Pinocchio in America, Allen Frost, 2019. After 82 years buried underground, Pinocchio returns to life behind a car repair shop in America.

Taking Her Sides on Immortality, Robert Huff, 2019. The long awaited poetry collection from a local, nationally renowned master of words.

Florida, Allen Frost, 2019. Three days in Florida turned into a book of sunshine inspired stories.

Blue Anthem Wailing, Allen Frost, 2019. My first novel written in college is an apocalyptic, Old Testament race through American shadows while Amelia Earhart flies overhead.

The Welfare Office, Allen Frost, 2019. The animals go in and out of the office, leaving these stories as footprints.

Island Air, Allen Frost, 2019. A detective novel featuring haiku, a lost library book and streetsongs.

Imaginary Someone, Allen Frost, 2020. A fictional memoir featuring 45 years of inspirations and obstacles in the life of a writer.

Violet of the Silent Movies, Allen Frost, 2020. A collection of starry-eyed short story poems, illustrated by the author.

The Tin Can Telephone, Allen Frost, 2020. A childhood memory novel set in 1975 Seattle, illustrated by author like a coloring book.

Heaven Crayon, Allen Frost, 2020. How the author's first book *Ohio Trio* would look if printed as a Big Little Book. Illustrated by the author.

Old Salt, Allen Frost, 2020. Authors of a fake novel get chased by tigers. Illustrations by the author.

A Field of Cabbages, Allen Frost, 2020. The sequel to *The Robotic Age* finds our heroes in a race against time to save Sunny Jim's ghost. Illustrated by Aaron Gunderson.

River Road, Allen Frost, 2020. A paperboy delivers the news to a ghost town. Illustrated by the author.

The Puttering Marvel, Allen Frost, 2021. Eleven short stories with illustrations by the author.

Something Bright, Allen Frost, 2021. 106 short story poems walking with you from winter into spring. Illustrated by the author.

The Trillium Witch, Allen Frost, 2021. A detective novel about witches in the Pacific Northwest rain. Illustrated by the author.

Cosmonaut, Allen Frost, 2021. Yuri Gagarin stars in this novel that follows his rocket landing in an American town. Midnight jazz, folk music, mystery and sorcery. Illustrated by the author.

Thriftstore Madonna, Allen Frost, 2021. 124 summer story poems. Illustrated by the author.

Half a Giraffe, Allen Frost, 2021. A magical novel about a counterfeiter and his unusual, beloved pet. Illustrated by the author.

Lexington Brown & The Pond Projector, Allen Frost, 2022. An underwater invention takes three friends through time. Illustrated by Aaron Gunderson.

The Robert Huck Museum, Allen Frost, 2022. The artist's life story told in photographs, woodcuts, paintings, prints and drawings.

Mrs. Magnusson & Friends, Allen Frost, 2022. A collection of 13 stories featuring mystery and magic and ginkgo leaves.

Magic Island, Allen Frost, 2022. There's a memory machine in this magic novel that takes us to college.

A Red Leaf Boat, Allen Frost, 2022. Inspired by Japan, this book of 142 poems is the result of walking in autumn.

Forest & Field, Allen Frost, 2022. 117 forest and field recordings made during the summer months, ending with a lullaby.

The Wires and Circuits of Earth, Allen Frost, 2022. 11 stories from a train station pulp magazine.

The Air Over Paris, Allen Frost, 2023. This novel reveals the truth about semi-sentient speedbumps from Mars.

Neptunalia, Allen Frost, 2023. A movie-novel for Neptune, featuring mystery in a Counterfeit Reality machine. Illustrated by Aaron Gunderson.

The Worrys, Allen Frost, 2023. A family of weasels look for a better life and get it. Illustrated by Tai Vugia.

American Mantra, Allen Frost, 2023. The future needs poetry to sleep at night. Only one man and one woman can save the world. Illustrated by Robert Huck.

One Drop in the Milky Way, Allen Frost, 2023. A novel about retiring, with a little help from a skeleton and Abraham Lincoln.

Follow Your Friend, Allen Frost, 2023. A collection of animals from sewn, stapled, and printed books spanning 34 years of writing.

Holograms from Mars, Allen Frost, 2024. Married Martians try to make do on Earth in this illustrated novel.

The Belateds, Allen Frost, 2024. The Belateds came to Seattle in 1964 and left the four chapters in this novel.

Jones Jr., Allen Frost, 2024. If you're a fan of 1970s television detectives, you'll be at home with this yarn.

Flop, Allen Frost, 2024. The B Minus Gallery presents a timeless work of art, while a seal goes out with the tide and pterodactyls spin in the sky.

Books by Bottom Dog Press

Ohio Trio, Allen Frost, 2001. Three short novels written in magic fields and small towns of Ohio. Reprinted as *Heaven Crayon* in 2020.

Bowl of Water, Allen Frost, 2004. Poetry. From the glass factory to when you wake up.

Another Life, Allen Frost, 2007. Poetry. From the last Ohio morning to the early bird.

Home Recordings, Allen Frost, 2009. Poetry. Dream machinery, filming Caruso, benign time travel.

The Mermaid Translation, Allen Frost, 2010. A bathysphere novel with Philip Marlowe.

Selected Correspondence of Kenneth Patchen, Edited by Larry Smith and Allen Frost, 2012. Amazing artist letters.

The Wonderful Stupid Man, Allen Frost, 2012. Short stories go from Aristotle's first car to the 500 dollar fool.